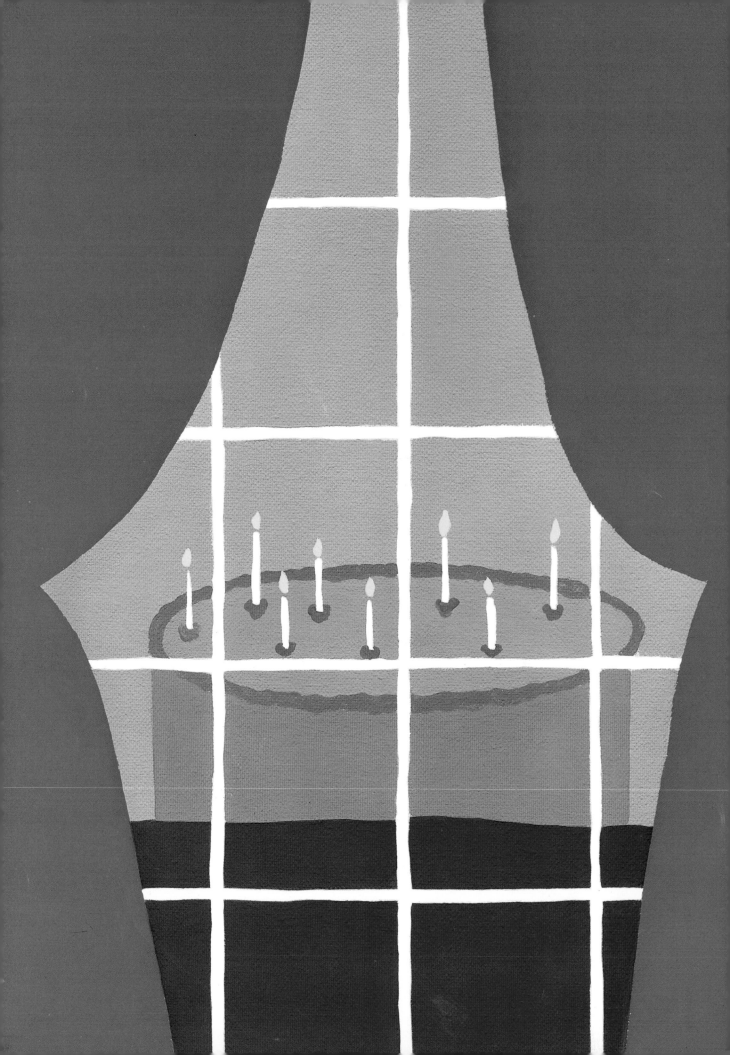

IT'S MY BIRTHDAY

Heidi Goennel

Tambourine Books
New York

ALLEN S HILL

The full-color illustrations were painted in acrylic on canvas.

Library of Congress Cataloging in Publication Data
Goennel, Heidi.   It's my birthday/Heidi Goennel.—1st ed.
p.   cm.
Summary: A child celebrates a birthday with a party,
long-distance telephone call, special card, cake, and gifts.
ISBN 0-688-11421-0 (trade.)—ISBN 0-688-11422-9 (lib. bdg.)
[1. Birthdays—Fiction.] I. Title.
PZ7.G554It   1992   [E]–dc20   91-30231   CIP   AC

1   3   5   7   9   10   8   6   4   2
First Edition

For my
mother and
father.

Guess what today is.

It's not the Fourth of July.

It's not Halloween.

It's my birthday. Now I'm a whole year older.

I just got a card from my friend Petey.
He lives far away now.

Nana has knitted a soft, new sweater for me. Uh oh.

Mommy and Daddy surprise me with a
new bicycle. WOW!

All my friends come to my party.

We play lots of games,

we go on pony rides,

and we dress up as pirates to hunt for
hidden treasure.

We watch a magician pull a real rabbit out of his hat.

Then we have ice cream and cake.
I make a big wish and blow out all the
candles. Happy Birthday!